The TRICKY TREATS

HALLOWEEN SPECIAL

Adaptation from the animated series: Robin Bright
Illustrations: Guru Animation Studio Ltd.

CRACKBOOM!

True and her friends put on their costumes: they're off to the Plumpkin Marsh! All year long, Tasty Treats have been growing inside every Plumpkin in the Rainbow Kingdom.

Today is the day the Plumpkins give them away!

"The Plumpkins are lighting up!" True exclaims.
"That means the Tasty Treats are ready!"
"Me first!" says Grizelda, approaching a Plumpkin.
"Treat, please."
But the Plumpkin shakes its head no.

"Remember, Grizelda?" True says. "You have to do something for the Plumpkin first." The Plumpkin nods excitedly. "Frookie," commands Grizelda. "Sit up and beg the Plumpkin for a Treat." But Frookie farts instead.

"No, like this!" says Grizelda. She pants and woof-woofs.
The Plumpkin thinks this is hilarious! Plop! It drops a Treat
in her basket. "Great job, Grizelda!" says True.
True and her friends proceed from Plumpkin to Plumpkin,
acting silly and collecting Treats.

As soon as they get home, True and Bartleby make a big pile of Treats! Bartleby reaches to try one.

"Wait!" True says. "We have to separate the Tasty Treats from the green Tricky Treats. Remember what the Rainbow King says? *Never eat a Tricky Treat. What happens next is not so sweet.*"

After sorting the Tricky Treats, Bartleby leaves them by the window. A moment later, they're gone! Looking out his window, he sees a Yeti carrying them away. "Those are bad Treats!" he cries. "Don't eat them!"

But the Yeti pops a Tricky Treat into his mouth.

Oh, no! The Yeti turns green all over.
His ears grow long and pointy like a wolf's.
His eyes glow red! And then he HOWLS.
He runs toward Rainbow City carrying all
of Bartleby's Tricky Treats.

Bartleby tells True what's happened.
"We have to stop him!" she says.

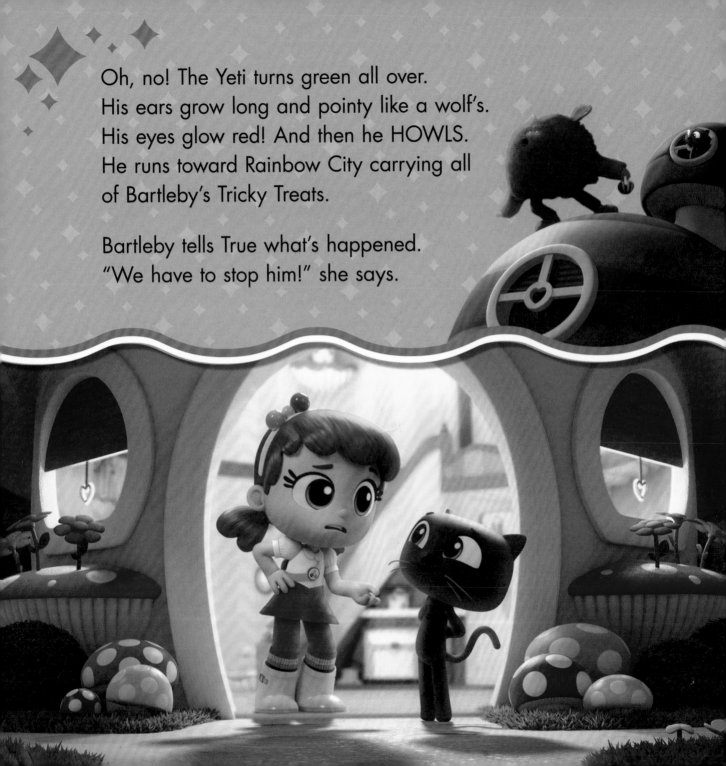

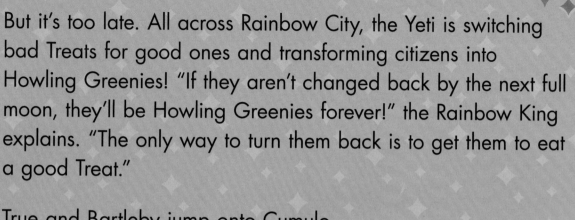

But it's too late. All across Rainbow City, the Yeti is switching bad Treats for good ones and transforming citizens into Howling Greenies! "If they aren't changed back by the next full moon, they'll be Howling Greenies forever!" the Rainbow King explains. "The only way to turn them back is to get them to eat a good Treat."

True and Bartleby jump onto Cumulo. "Time for Wish help!" she says.

"Zee," True says at the Wishing Tree. "We need your help. All the citizens of the Rainbow Kingdom are turning into Howling Greenies! We have to change them back before the moon is full."

"Let's sit and have a think about this," Zee says.

True and Zee sit down on the mushrooms. They each take a deep breath. True says, "I need a Wish that can help me gather together all the Greenies right away… and prevent me from turning into one myself! Then I need to get them all to eat a Tasty Treat."

"The Wishing Tree has heard you, True," Zee says.
"It's time to get your three Wishes."

WISHING TREE,
WISHING TREE,
PLEASE SHARE YOUR WONDERFUL
WISHES WITH ME.

The Wishes wake up and spin around True.
Three Wishes stay with her, and the others return
to the Wishing Tree.

"Very interesting Wishes," Zee says.
"I can tell you more about their powers.
Let's check the Wishopedia."

BUBBLO
keeps you safe inside
your own bubble.

FLINGO
launches things into
the air.

SHARESIE
helps you share
things with others.

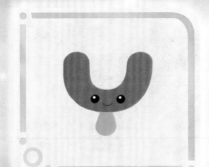
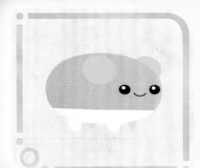

"Thank you, Zee. And thank you,
Wishing Tree, for sharing your
Wishes with me," True says, as
she leaves with the Wishes in
her pack.

Back in Rainbow City, things have gotten even worse: Frookie has been tricked into eating a bad Treat, and now he's a Howling Greenie too!

The Greenies surround True and her friends. They're closing in! "Time for my first Wish!" True says.

ZIP ZAP ZOO!

"Bubblo, protect us from the Howling Greenies!" says True. True, Bartleby, and Grizelda are each surrounded by a bubble, keeping them safe. What a relief!

Once the Greenies are gone, True throws Frookie a good Treat. He jumps and gobbles it up. When he lands, he's back to his normal self!

Together, True and her friends have just enough good Treats to save every citizen of Rainbow City. "But the Greenies are spread all over," Bartleby says. "How will we get a Treat to each of them?"

True has an idea: "Remember how Frookie caught the Treat we tossed him? Maybe the others will too, if Flingo helps us!"

True activates her second Wish.

ZIP ZAP ZOO!

Flingo launches the good Treats into the air. The Greenies catch them in their mouths, just like Frookie did! One by one, the Greenies turn back into citizens. One even turns back into the Yeti!

A full moon rises over Rainbow City—and there aren't any Howling Greenies left! "The good news is that thanks to you, the citizens are safe," says the Rainbow King.

"The bad news is that all the Treats are gone. I hope you're not too disappointed."

This is terrible news. Bartleby can't believe it.
"There aren't any Treats anywhere?" says
Bartleby.
"Sorry, Bee," True says. "Only this one little
wee one."
"You mean I have to wait a whole year
until next Plumpkin Day?" he says.

"Wait!" says True. "I forgot! I still have my third Wish. Let's see what Sharesie can do!"

"Wake up, Sharesie. Wish come true! Can you help us share this one little Treat with the whole Rainbow Kingdom?"

Sharesie makes a happy sound. A moment later, a shower of Treats falls from the sky.

"Awesome!" says True. "Thanks, Sharesie."
"Wait!" says Bartleby. "We need to sort these Treats! Everyone knows to *Never eat a Tricky Treat!*"

CrackBoom! Books is an imprint of Chouette Publishing (1987) Inc.

Text: adaptation by Robin Bright of the animated series TRUE AND THE RAINBOW KINGDOM™/MC,
produced by Guru Studio.
Original script written by Steve Westren
Original episode #404: Tricky Treat Day
All rights reserved.

Illustrations: © GURU STUDIO. All Rights Reserved.

Chouette Publishing would like to thank the Government of Canada and SODEC
for their financial support.

Bibliothèque et Archives nationales du Québec and Library and Archives
Canada cataloguing in publication

Title: The tricky treats: Halloween special/adaptation, Robin Bright; illustrations,
Guru Studios.
Names: Bright, Robin, 1966- author. | Guru Studio (Firm), illustrator.
Description: Series statement: True and the Rainbow Kingdom
Identifiers: Canadiana 20200079999 | ISBN 9782898021169 (softcover)
Classification: LCC PZ7.1.B75 Tr 2020 | DDC j813/.6—dc23

Legal deposit – Bibliothèque et Archives nationales du Québec, 2020.
Legal deposit – Library and Archives Canada, 2020.

Printed in Canada
10 9 8 7 6 5 4 3 2 1   CHO2094 MAY2020